I'M NOT YOUR SLAVE

THE STORY OF IMTIYAAZ

ERIC REESE

ISBN: 978-1-925988-04-8

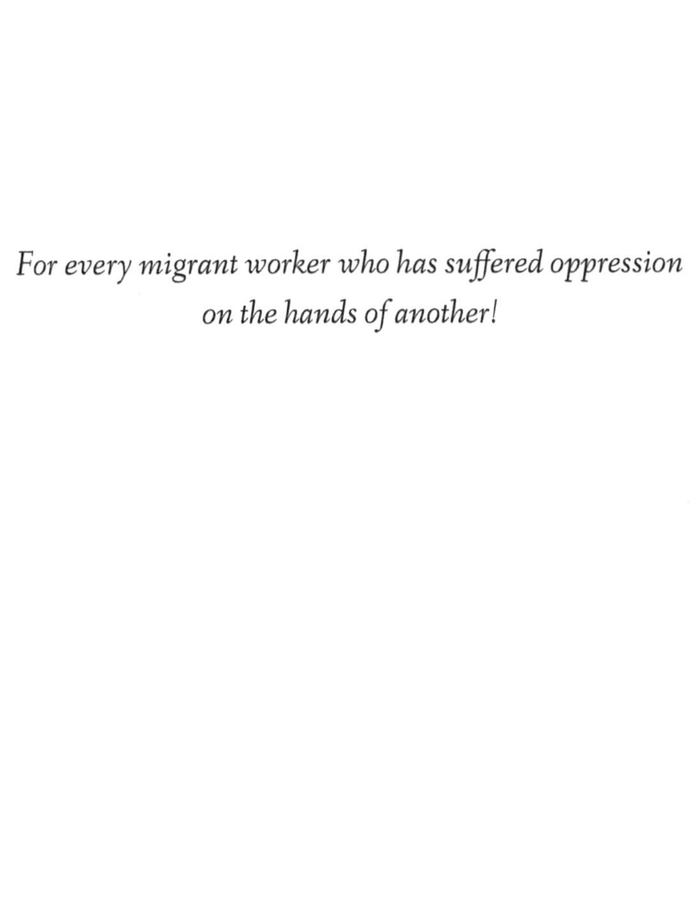

For every migrant worker who has suffered oppression on the hands of another!

"Our lives begin to end the day we become silent about the things that matter."

MARTIN LUTHER KING, JR.

CONTENTS

The check-in at Jakarta International Airport for the five o'clock Emirates Airlines flight to the UAE was light for a Friday afternoon. Everyone looked exhausted, and it appeared passengers were heading back to the UAE for some much-needed rest except for one person. Imtiyaaz easily stood out as the only passenger who wasn't wearied by whatever seemed to wear people out about Jakarta. While most passengers had cheap bags or simple carry-ons, Imtiyaaz was carrying a Louis Vuitton Monogram Train Case with her cosmetics inside her Celine Tri-Fold leather handbag. She was eager to leave Indonesia behind and everything it held for her. To be fair, it wasn't much: a grumpy father who had never stopped blaming her for being the reason her mother had dead, a few network of friends, and Sayyid Yacob, a close friend of the family.

Ahead of her in line, stood a tall, fit black Emirati male with a stylish heavy beard. Imtiyaaz, who stood behind the towering hunk, had spent minutes, staring his impressive physique. She silently hoped he'd sit next to her on the flight.

Her oversized silver sunglasses ensured she could eyeball the sexy hunk without detection even if he turned around. Imtiyaaz's mind then drifted to the new life awaiting her at the other end of this journey.

Ordinarily, on most days, like this Friday, since finishing high school, Imtiyaaz worked in a small restaurant making coffee and waiting tables. The Arabs tipped better than her countrymen, and it was here where she'd first nursed the vision of living and working in one of the oil-rich Gulf countries. UAE was top on her list of countries to work in and Saudi Arabia being the bottom. After close to two years of nursing her dreams while schooling in the day and working in the evenings, Imtiyaaz was finally moving along in the right direction.

At first, she'd considered applying for university

abroad, but figured it was better to work first. With a father like hers, it was a brilliant idea to say at least.

* * *

One day, fate had smiled on her when a regular customer at the shop, Aisyah, half-Qatari and half-Indonesian, had told her of jobs in the UAE. Aisyah had lived in Dubai when she was younger.

"It is perfect for girls like you," said Aisyah smiling.

"What do you mean by perfect for girls like me?" asked, Imitiyaaz curious to know.

"Oh, I meant you know how you are working here. It's the same but you get paid more money there. People like Asian ladies there. They are so polite," stuttered Aisyah unable to speak English very well.

Quick to smile and tip generously, Aisyah had easily became Imtiyaaz's favorite customer. They would have long chats while Aisyah ate about Dubai, especially on days when the manager wasn't around. Aisyah told Imtiyaaz she was double majoring in Political Science and Far-East Asian Studies. Once she finished her research paper at the end of the term, she'd be graduating and leaving Jakarta for good.

Imtiyaaz learned about a recruiting agency in the UAE for hospitality jobs in one of those chats with Aisyah. She told Imtiyaaz that she could pass her CV along to one of her colleagues there in hopes of getting hired.

"You know with the Emirates being a top tourist destination in the Middle East, hospitality businesses are springing up left and right. They need energetic, bright girls like you and me, Imtiyaaz."

Imtiyaaz found Aisyah's assessment of her endearing and wished it was the same confidence her father could give her just for a day. But not Arief; he was always complaining, and that's when he even bothered to speak. Sometimes, Imtiyaaz and her father would go weeks without saying a word to each other. He'd mumble to her greetings or give little praise for something she did well.

Imtiyaaz, after giving Aisyah her CV, spent time asking her closest friend, Sayyida her thoughts about her working in the Middle East.

"I don't think it's wise to leave Jakarta and go to another country where you don't know anyone. I read stories in the paper all the time and heard on the news about many cases of human trafficking over there and it's sickening. Plus, some of our citizens who worked as maids over there got tortured and killed."

And Sayyida wasn't the only one to tell Imtiyaaz this. Her friend Dewi and Nadia said the same. This left Imtiyaaz wondering why it seemed like everyone was telling her it was a bad idea.

"We have to take our chances or die in poverty, Sayyida. The grass is greener there, and I'm still a teenager. I can work for a few years, save money and help out here. We should want something more than just working in retail or restaurants, right?"And that was Imitiyaaz's generic response – with slight adjustments, depending on which person she was talking to.

"Excuse me, excuse me." A gruff voice coming from behind startled everyone in line.

Imtiyaaz turned to see an average height blonde man in blazers eyeing her. The guy looked like a college boy with his nerdy hip glasses, flowery shirt and expensive loafers. He pointed to the space in front of Imtiyaaz who had been daydreaming, so she slowly moved up.

"Sorry."

"No problem, sweetheart."

"Am I the one making a mistake?" thought Imtiyaaz, rolling her eyes as she turned back around.

The man was talking on his phone bragging. Imtiyaaz listened closely to his conversation; he was a fashion design student at the Corcoran School of the Arts and Design in Washington, DC. He flew to Jakarta then to UAE for a fashion expo. As the man kept blabbering, he kept looking over at Imtiyaaz; pinpointing every item she had from her train case, handbag to her sunglasses.

"A pair of black Giuseppe Zanotti Cruel Summer sandals, black Hudson distressed skinny jeans, over-sized white button-up shirt and black Chanel J12 Automatic 38mm watch," he said to whoever he was talking to on the phone, right in front of Imtiyaaz without reservation. "Hey, Richard. I'm telling you this girl's amazing. I have to write about this in my next blog. I didn't know Indonesian women had style like this."

"Her make-up is flawless. *She might be wearing NARS or Make Up Forever.* "Ha!" he gasped betting his last cent mentally he was right. "Yeah, Richard. She's wearing Marc Yacob's Decadence, too. My God! Where did she come from? Ok, pal. I'll see you when I get back. See ya!" The college boy then hung up the phone.

Imtiyaaz, sighed *"finally"* while moving up a few steps. She then smiled at the agent at the scanner as she passed through, not aware that removal of shoes, belts and electronics was mandatory. It was Imtiyaaz's first time inside an airport although she had her passport for two years. As she neared the waiting area, there were different flights over the loudspeaker being announced. *Where is that cute Arab guy? He's right there at Starbucks, and the stools beside him are all taken.* Imtiyaaz pouted, knowing that she had her chance.

Imtiyaaz sat near the flight dashboard and saw her flight light up in orange before it was announced. EMIRATES FLIGHT 798 TO THE UAE LEAVING JAKARTA HAS NOW BEEN DELAYED FOR TWO HOURS. As the announcement came in, Imtiyaaz overheard someone talking on their phone mentioning that there was a sandstorm in the UAE and all flights scheduled there were being delayed. Moments later, she felt a faint buzz in her handbag.

"Hello."

"Hello, Ms Imtiyaaz."

It was a male voice which sounded like the recruiter, Mr Ismael.

"Hi, Mr Ismael. I'm at the airport. Our flight's delayed for two hours probably because there's a sandstorm. That's what I'm hearing."

"Okay. See you soon."

"Hopefully, it won't be a problem."

"No, it's fine."

"Have the others arrived yet?"

"Sorry, but I don't have that information. You'll see them when you get here. I have to go. Your porter will pick you up once you arrive and maybe I'll be there, too. Look out for the driver who will be holding up your name placard. Masalama."

Imtiyaaz wondered if she had said something wrong.

"Okay, Mr Ismael—"

Then, the phone line was cut off.

"That's weird," thought Imtiyaaz.

She took out a book, *The Boy Toys of Paris* she'd packed and wanted to read badly, opening it while waiting for her flight number to be finally called.

It's been a long two hours, and the flight to Dubai was finally ready to depart. She clung onto her hand luggage thinking about the bigger bags that had been checked in. *"Please don't lose my stuff,"* she thought as the flight attendants were giving safety instructions. She was seated between the blond college fashion freak and a brunette woman in her mid-thirties.

Once the plane cleared the airspace and the seat-belt sign beeped, Imtiyaaz opened up Instagram on her phone and checked her notifications. The guy and brunette kept peeking at her photo-shopped photos on Instagram next to famous American celebrities. Imtiyaaz had learned Photoshop from her friend, Hamid and enjoyed making spoofs in her spare time. Her captions were written in the line of, "This is a dream, so please mind my space."

Many of Imtiyaaz's friends called her conceited but it was that vanity that pushed her forward. She knew one day she'd prove them wrong. Imtiyaaz then started commenting; first with a picture she had with Porsha Williams of Housewives of Atlanta. Then, one with Eva Longoria and Janelle Monae and another with her, Kevin Hart and Dwayne Johnson posing on the red carpet. Her favorite was the one she had with Colin Farrell laughing beside her while eating at a famous restaurant.

Imtiyaaz had enough of the brunette constantly looking, so she turned off her phone and began thinking about everything that had brought her to this point.

CHAPTER 2

The space from one finger to the next wasn't empty. Arief filled it, locking their hands together. He held onto Fatima's as tightly as he could and wasn't ready to let her hand go neither was he going to look away. Beads of sweat were forming on his wife's face and Arief wasn't spared in the sweat-bath either as he screamed when she did.

"Sayang, you can do it." Their hands clasped together, her teeth clenched and face frowned as she pushed; a baby girl was born, and its cry filled the room. "We did it, Sayang. We did it!"

"Congratulations! We'll give you both a few minutes with your child," said the doctor walking out with the nurses.

Arief was too excited to describe the joy of having his first child. His laughter was glorious but after a few minutes, it didn't last when he looked down. Fatima's smile was weakening and her eyes were closing and opening. *Something was wrong.* She didn't say a word except for "*Cintaku.*"

The sound of drops from the IV hit the hospital floor. Arief followed the sound with his eyes only to discover that the IV was punctured. Her hands were melting like palm oil in his. Arief tried cupping her face, but as close as he was, Fatima seemed so distanced.

The harder he tried squeezing, the further her soul seemed fading away. The color of her face began fading away. Arief let out a loud cry; one desperately seeking help but no one answered. If he could summon anyone, just anyone without letting Fatima go, he'd do so, however the doctors and nurses were too far away.

The cry of little Imtiyaaz grew louder, deafening Arief's ears. Arief quickly responded, turning towards the room's door. There were doctors standing down the hall but they weren't paying attention to his frantic call for help. Arief ran back inside, searching for the baby, but couldn't find it, yet its cry grew louder and louder. He tried screaming but something was blocking his voice. The hospital room felt as if it was closing in on him as the alarm sounded, waking the old man out of latest nightmare.

Thankful, Arief opened his eyes and said Al-Hamdulilah. The jolt back to reality was what Arief needed whenever he saw this dream. It was dawn, and as he stumbled to get up, he accidentally cursed, disgusted by the mess on the bed that blocked his way. His shirt was dripping from sweat and while trying to get his head straight, Arief bumped into a stool near the bathroom.

"Damn it." Arief held his head instead of his knee, confused about his pain as he limped over to the window and pulled the curtains apart. The faint sunlight that entered inside gave the old man an-all clear that remnants of tonight's nightmare was fading away.

"I can't handle these nightmares much longer," Arief mumbled as he squinted a few more times.

Arief then looked down at his shirt, and after, up at the ceiling fan which at its highest speed, yet his sweat showed the contrast. He stretched, before cracking his knuckles and took off his shirt and tossed it in the pile of clutter that began four days ago.

The green sheet on his bed was faded and help-lessly calling to be washed. There were dirty and clean clothes mixed together on the floor and bed and even the bedposts were not spared. Then, Arief remembered the promise he made to repaint the room but the old man said this week after week. The cracks on the ceiling and paint chips on the ground were increasing, yet, he kept putting it off. Actually, the last time the house was in tip-top shape was when Imtiyaaz was three. Arief couldn't remember, like anything else that was detailed but often believed that it was around Imtiyaaz's fourth or fifth birthday.

The only thing Arief had polished regularly and treasured in the room was a portrait of Fatima sitting on a tree stump with a cat on her lap. Laughing, a person could tell from the photograph that she passed away happy. She had black and big eyes which stressed every feature of her cute little face. On a table nearby, was another portrait that Fatima took with Arief weeks before her death. They were smiling heavily in the middle of a radiant spring day.

Even now, as Arief looked over his room, he smiled for the happy memories. "I miss you sweetheart," he wished Fatima heard and answered. He touched the portrait and sighed at the realisation of what was decreed long ago, *"She's gone to Allah,*

Arief." At that moment, Arief came to his senses realising it was time to get ready for his day.

Imtiyaaz heard in the middle of the night when her father screamed and knew it was one of his nightmares again. She also knew never to go to his room; knowing that better than any of her father's rules. "You're *a stupid kid that destroyed my life.*" That was what he told Imtiyaaz the time she offered to help, and that was around three years ago. She went on about her business pretending he'd never said it but it hurt her. In her younger years, Arief had often warned her about coming inside especially on the day that she got caught playing in her mother's makeup kit.

As Imtiyaaz prepared Bubur Ayam; an entree she'd learned to make well from working, she kept dozing off. She'd been awake since Fajr, trying to straighten up the house. When she checked the time, and it was 8:00. Her father started work at 8:30 and usually left around a quarter after eight. Imtiyaaz waited anxiously for him to leave, so she could go back to sleep, but her father was taking his time this morning. She readied his food and brought out a tray and condiments to the sitting room. Consciously, Imtiyaaz checked to make sure everything was perfect, not wanting to hear her father complain. Then she sat, opening and closing her eyes briefly at the slightest creak. She didn't want her father to catch her resting.

And itt was a routine for this young woman to be up by six because her father often signalled that if she wanted a roof over her head, make sure she was up. It was easier back when she was in high school two years ago. Nowadays, not so much. Imityaaz has a problem with oversleeping and her father usually yells her name to wake her for Fajr. As she waited for her father to come out, she heard the *"You got mail"* notification from her laptop in the other room. She'd been applying for better paying jobs since graduation. She tries to sneak back to her room but bumps into her father and about faces.

"Salam alaykum. Sorry ayah. Morning, ayah."

He sighed as she led the way to the sitting room. Through it, was a small kitchen which resembled the back of a pizzeria with its large hole in the wall extending out to the front. The view gave the impression of customers being watched coming in and out. As Imtiyaaz carried her father's breakfast, she watched him fixing the TV. He remained there for over a minute trying to adjust the antenna as Imtiyaaz noticed his hair had grown too long. *Papa needs a haircut.* His beard was also growing too thick; the split ends of its hairs were breaking off, making him look unattractive. Arief was a tall muscular man, who often worked out at the local gym with Sayyid Yacob when Sayyid was here. Now that Sayyid is in Saudia Arabia, he'd stop going. The limp from an accident last year coming home from a karaoke bar was the excuse he often used in saying why he wasn't working out often. However, that accident did not stop him from singing on the weekends. Imtiyaaz always thought that by her father openly bragging about his accident to his friends often was a sign that he wanted to leave this world.

Imtiyaaz looked away quickly as she didn't want her father to catch her staring. Shortly after handing him his breakfast, she filled a metal cup with water and placed it in front of him. Meanwhile, Arief was more focused on the news then his daughter and while both didn't say a word to each other, Imtiyaaz just sat there and watched along.

Sayyid Yacob, a friend of the family for as long as Imtiyaaz could remember was more of a father-figure to her than Arief. He was two years younger than Arief and lived in the next compound before he married and went to Saudi Arabia. When people found out Arief was her father, they were shocked, believing it was Sayyid. Mr Yacob assumed the role of parent at Imtiyaaz's sports events, parent-teacher meetings, and Sepak Takraw competitions. He would also take Imtiyaaz to the mosque on Fridays if her father was too busy working. Then after prayers, they'd go out for ice cream at Plaza Indonesia.

Sayyid Yacob shared everything with Imtiyaaz and told her to follow her dreams no matter where it will lead her. On Saturdays when Imtiyaaz was younger, she'd go with him to his farm to help out. He would allow her to truss the hay and they'd ride horses in the fields that his father left behind. With Sayyid Yacob away working in Saudi Arabia, Imtiyaaz feels lonely most days.

The last time they spoke, he told her he was enjoying life there, praying at Masjid Haram and hoped she'll be able to visit one day. Imtiyaaz dearly missed him, reflecting on their past while squeezing the bracelet he had given her during the last Hari Raya Puasa holiday as her father ate.

"I'm off to work," said Arief, snapping Imtiyaaz out of her daydream.

She didn't even notice he had finished and before Imtiyaaz could complete her sentence — "Okay, goodbye ayah," he was out the door. Left behind only, was an empty plate on the wooden chair. Imtiyaaz then turned off the TV while staring at the picture frame of her deceased mother.

"This man loves you more than me. I'll never understand why but you must have been his only true friend," ponders Imtiyaaz.

Imtiyaaz didn't hear the details of her mother's death through a father-daughter conversation, but through her father's rants which pointed to her being responsible. Fatima was his heart but Imtiyaaz is her mother's only child. Not only did Arief know this it, but her looks confirmed it; the same color hair, big black eyes, nose and small mouth.

You got mail. Imtiyaaz rushed to her room to check. After overcoming a non-clicking mouse pad, she opened it and the message was from a local retail company. *A job in sales, really.* Imtiyaaz shook her head in disappointment; working home was her last preference. Imtiyaaz applied for that position over four months ago, so she could get away from her father. Now, she wants to leave home for good.

Imtiyaaz sighed in confusion but was willing to take a chance, a risk to wait it out; even if the others wouldn't reply. It was a risk they preached in the local mosque she attended, *"Put your trust in Allah."*

Imtiyaaz went back to bed after cleaning up; needing every inch of sleep before resuming work at 2pm. Her sleep was interrupted slightly because the eighteen-year-old forgot to wash her uniform.

Imtiyaaz's workplace was like home and she enjoyed every moment of it; savouring the interactions with daily regular customers. The warmth atmosphere of brewing coffee and little shop's hippie environment gave her a rare awesomeness. Imtiyaaz didn't get that feeling anywhere else in Jakarta.

The coffee shop/restaurant was located in Tibet Timur in South Jakarta. Imtiyaaz usually took GRAB from home to get there or if there was more time, she'd take the train to Tebet Station, then walk. She recognised every face that came since most of the customers were locals. The management applauded her being so kind that they secretly gave her a raise twice in three months and Imtiyaaz was grateful.

"How long will it take you to fall in love with me?"

Imtiyaaz heard a gentleman's voice, not far from the shop's counter. She had her back turned, brewing coffee but knew who it was. That sentiment made her smile. Yet, she didn't say anything until she was finished with a customer. The gentleman didn't bother leaving; standing there and watching as Imtiyaaz did her work.

"Hello, Hamid. Salam alaykum. What can I get you this afternoon?" Imtiyaaz teased him as they had a little playful thing going on now for months.

"Well, I'll have my usual." She smiled at the twenty-two-year-old Egyptian. His English was broken as he mixed Egyptian words while speaking. But Imtiyaaz liked it; it made her smile, especially when he told her he was in love with her. Not only did it shock her, she actually was falling for his charm. Hamid was in Indonesia as a part-time university student and part-time traveler. His parents appeared to support his adventures. Most of the time while in Indonesia, he went sightseeing and was fascinated by the tourists' attractions such as Grand Mall Indonesia, the National Monument,

Taman Mini Indonesia Indah, and of course, Bali. Since he was a child, he told Imtiyaaz he always wanted to visit these places and had a list of others he had his sights set on. Hamid raved about the pictures he'd taken while traveling, but also told Imtiyaaz that pictures weren't good except for the ones of non-living objects. Imtiyaaz learned a lot about Islam while talking with him. He had even taught Imtiyaaz Photoshop and that's how she learned how to make awesome memes.

Just last week, as the sun was setting and Hamid was leaving his friend's shop a few stores down, he ran back inside Imtiyaaz's workplace and carried Imtiyaaz outside. All he wanted was to show her the sky. Its colour was torn between blue and orange and the sight was quite beautiful. Hamid snapped a few pictures of Imtiyaaz, impressing Imtiyaaz by each snapshot.

They had known each other only three weeks, but instantly clicked. Her charismatic boldness and friendliness, along with his charm and never-ending stories were a match made in heaven. Hamid told her about his journeys to Mount Bromo, Torajaland and The Borobudur.

"I will not stop travelling until I die," said Hamid often.

"Take me with you," was Imtiyaaz's response jokingly knowing her father would never approve.

"In-sha-Allah."

Hamid's next stop was China to take photos of what left of the Great Wall. He also wanted to walk its length. He'd asked Imtiyaaz numerous times to come along, but she declined every time. And still Hamid would ask, and she would continue to decline. Whenever Imtiyaaz saw Hamid, it renewed her faith and determination to follow her fantasies.

***

"Your favourite cheesy turkey scrolls are coming up." Imtiyaaz said, winking while writing down his total on a sticky note.

"Marry me and I'll show you the world," Hamid teased as always.

"You'll take me to Egypt?"

"Wherever dost thou want?" Hamid said taking a bow.

Imtiyaaz laughed at his attempt to use Shakespearean words with his strong accent.

"I shall take thou, Oh beautiful princess to the Great Sphinx of Giza and to the lands of Luxor. You just say in this ear of mine where thou hast in mind, and I shall make it come true."

Imtiyaaz grabbed the ends of the table, laughing, "Oh Hamid, you're so sweet."

"I take you have fallen in love with me?" Hamid replied with feigned amusement in his eyes.

"Oh well, you are lovely, sweetie. I can't imagine who wouldn't fall in love with you. But one thing's for sure now, my dear Hamid, you're not going to get me fired today."

Hamid held his hands up and backed away. "I'll be at the table waiting. Please, add a cup of small coffee to that order with extra milk and sukoor."

"Of course. By the way, what is sukoor? You always say this word."

"Sugar. In Egypt, we say sukoor."

"Oh, okay."

Imtiyaaz just couldn't stop her lips from curling up. The handsome young Egyptian was just too sweet and it affected not only her but every customer that walked inside. Imtiyaaz watched him once play with a little girl, making her constantly laugh from his clownish gestures. He got the family to laugh along.

Imtiyaaz went back to work and her phone beeped inside her apron's pocket. Hoping that the perfect job would contact her, her brows dropped when she saw that it was just a message from Telkomsel, reminding her she should renew her data or else service would be cut.

Diah brought Hamid's order out along with some others. She was a cook but did more than one job. The shop's owner, Mr Razzaq owes everything to her. Diah had a passion for cooking, and Imtiyaaz learned a lot from her. She taught Imtiyaaz about different ways to make good Nasi platters, and it was one of the saving graces her father really enjoyed.

Diah, although working at the coffee shop the longest, didn't make a lot of money and there were times where she could have if she had only left. Her low self-esteem is what held her back. Diah had a few chances to be featured in some Southeast Asia's biggest cooking competitions but always backed out at the last minute. Diah's excuse was that other competitors were better than her.

Imtiyaaz wished she had the same chance as she looked at the dishes that Diah put on the counter. Without words, she signalled to Diah to help. Diah looked at every plate, hissed and carried only two. Imtiyaaz looked down at the four remaining, while Elok, Diah's helper, was bringing out more. Imtiyaaz swallowed her pride and grabbed what she could, putting on an array of smiles to the customers waiting. Those smiles were only ushered in when the world wondered who Imtiyaaz really was.

The last smile of the day made everyone think everything was going well with her, but she was not. She didn't have to beg her inner self to show it. When she needed it the most, it came quickly and freely but disappeared once the delights had faded. It was her job to keep the customers happy and Imtiyaaz displayed that while making sure that she remained focused on her future.

The shop closed at 11pm, but Imtiyaaz usually left by 10:30, having to be home by 11:15, or else her father wouldn't open the door. It was Arief's golden rule and Imtiyaaz made sure that she complied. Once, she arrived at 11:21pm, knocked hard, begging her father to open the door, but he didn't. She didn't ask her neighbours to help, so she slept at the nearby mosque. Her father was more friendly with his friends than Imtiyaaz. When they come over, Arief was the happiest, singing and yelling while watching the football matches. Imtiyaaz checked her phone, seeing it was 10:37, "Oh my

God!" Imtiyaaz gathered her things and was out the door, waiting for her GRAB ride in front of the shop. Hopefully, she won't be late or else.

***

Imtiyaaz arrived faster than expected and told the driver to let her off at the Indomaret. Outside, she saw a beggar with a bowl and cane, so she dropped some rupiah in his dirty bowl. The man looked worn out and besides him was an old sleeping bag. Imtiyaaz looked at the man again and gave him 500000 rupiah. The man made prayers for her and she did the same in return.

Imtiyaaz's phone buzzed once she got home and she wasn't eager to take it out. It was another message from her service provider again. As she was about to put the phone back in her pocket, it buzzed again; a message from Sayyid Yacob came in first. As she was about to read it, another message followed.

"Hey my dear. How are you? In school yet? I miss you and Arief. If you need anything, let me know. I'll call soon."

Imtiyaaz smiled attempting to reply, but remembered that she didn't have no more credit.

The second text was from Layla, a woman she

sometimes babysat for. *We need you on Saturday.* Imtiyaaz was thrilled as Layla paid well, sometimes more than her salary from the coffee shop. She was about to reply but she forgot to buy data at the store. The message from Layla gave Imtiyaaz much hope, and she thanked Allah for it. Now, she can rest despite sleeping in a home that has dark clouds hovering over it.

Imtiyaaz came back to her senses by turbulence. She looked up at her aisle's dashboard and read 30 *minutes to arrival.* Imtiyaaz wondered what the two passengers, she was sandwiched between, will be doing once they arrive to the UAE. *Were they looking forward to a new life like me?* From the looks of the other passengers' faces, it seemed as if no one was looked happy.

Regardless, Imtiyaaz couldn't wait to get off the plane walk through the sands of the United Arab Emirates. The pilot announced over the intercom they will arriving at Abu Dhabi International Airport in about twenty minutes. That announcement gave Imtiyaaz a boost of confidence signalling she was headed in the right direction.

Imtiyaaz stood in the immigration line waiting to be processed and then followed the cue pointing in the direction of Arrivals. As she walked, she saw many nationalities; Arabs, Asians, Europeans and Africans.

"Wow! There are so many foreigners here," she thought as she looked around for a man holding a placard with her name on it. Imtiyaaz didn't see anyone, so she headed over to the baggage claim; noticing that she might have overdressed. Locals were staring at her as if she was a celebrity and Imtiyaaz found it quite strange. "Perhaps, it was better for me to dress as someone poor," she thought. However, the younger ladies were admiring her style especially the way her khimar matched perfectly. But it was while Imtiyaaz was heading for the exit, someone called out her name.

"Ms Imtiyaaz!"

She turned around, seeing a short stocky man wearing a plaid shirt resembling someone of Indian descent.

"Yes. And you are?"

"Ms Imtiyaaz. I am your porter, Hajji. I'll take your things to the car outside. The men are waiting for you. Welcome to the UAE. I hope you had a good flight."

The man looked at my bags curiously as he spoke as if he was trying to decide which one weighed the most.

"What men?" asked Imtiyaaz.

"The Arbaab."

"I never heard this word before. Can you explain?

"Oh sorry. I meant the bosses. They're called Arbaab in Arabic."

"Oh, okay. I guess I'll have to learn Arabic then. What an interesting name?"

Imtiyaaz didn't like his slick hair and the cheap perfume the man was wearing. As they walked over to the parking area, the Indian man tried making small talk but Imtiyaaz had very little to say. Ahead, there was a red 2018 Humvee with two Arabs dressed in white smoking cigarettes chatting. One man greeted her introducing himself as Mr Ismael while the other kept looking.

"Hi, my dear, Imtiyaaz. You're welcome to the UAE," he said in broken English. "We'll take you to where you'll be staying for tonight."

"It's a pleasure to meet you, Mr Ismael. Thank

you for the opportunity." Imtiyaaz went to shake his hand but he refused.

"No worries, my dear. Here in our culture we don't shake women's hands but the pleasure's the same."

"Ok. I didn't know. I'm sorry."

Imtiyaaz watched the Indian get into the driver's seat after taking her bags to a second car beside the Humvee. Imtiyaaz didn't recognise its model but knew it was costs a lot of money.

"Don't worry, my dear. Your belongings are safe. Our guys know the location. By the way, how was your flight?" said Mr Ismael when he saw Imtiyaaz's face.

"Not bad. Al hamdulilah. I was boxed in between two people from two different regions of the world. It was interesting, say to least."

"Al hamdulilah. You're Muslim?"

"Yes, Mr Ismael."

"Al hamdulilah."

"Yallah!" Mr Ismael then yelled to the Indian who was starting the vehicle.

Imtiyaaz got inside and the second man who was smoking with Mr Ismael, got in the blue sports car beside it. For close to ten minutes, inside Abu Dhabi's airport terminal, both vehicles followed each other, bumper to bumper. Imtiyaaz, in the meantime, kept watching the blue sports car through the rear-view mirror, wondering if the man would get lost; causing her to lose her precious personals.

"I've been wondering about the sandstorm that caused my flight to delay," said Imtiyaaz trying to make small talk.

"It's usually not in the habit of waiting around for everyone to see it," said Mr Ismael cockily.

Imtiyaaz got Mr Ismael's sarcasm, so she sat back and relaxed while the AC was blasting. The city was so beautiful as its sands surrounded civilization. The heat was penetrating through the car's metal and Mr Ismael kept telling the driver to hurry. As they drove up the long highway known as Shaikh Zayed Road, Imtiyaaz pondered how people could make such a beautiful place out of a desert.

CHAPTER 3

Arief had to make breakfast now that Imtiyaaz was abroad. He was upset with himself for letting her go. For two days in a row, he tried making Nasi Kambing, only to end up throwing it away. On the third day, he simply gave up.

"Stupid Kambing." Arief sighed as he carried whatever looked eatable with him and a glass of water to the sitting room. He wanted Telur with it, but didn't have the patience to keep cooking. It was a beautiful Saturday morning with the sun rising gracefully except that Arief didn't think so. He ate on the floor, with his legs crossed, not realising he was in front of Fatima's portrait until he had finished. Arief missed not having his wife around.

Suddenly, the pan of leftover rice dropped onto the wooden floor while he was standing up. The sound of the metal against the wood was more irritating than the mess. The old man didn't care with his mind being one thing; Fatima.

"Fatima," he weeped.

A tear dropped and others followed. He took down the portrait and held it in his arms dearly; weeping so bitterly and trembling like an erupting volcano.

The memories they shared flooded his senses making him cry more and more. They had met at his uncle's farm in the village about twenty years ago. She had come with a friend who was working on his uncle's field. The first time Fatima spoke, it captivated Arief and her constant giggles when she tried mounting a horse and fell off. The fall wasn't hard; but what was amusing was how she laughed after the fall. The field workers ran to her aid and she kept saying she was okay. More than once that same day, she tried mounting the same horse.

Arief tried offering her help, but Fatima said that she could do it. Her determination was enough for Arief to watch from a distance, making sure she wouldn't kill herself. Fatima then soothed the horse for the twentieth time and whispered in her ears and even laughed at it frequently. Arief somehow was enjoying the moment and felt compelled to guard this young woman from harm. Fatima didn't stop trying and ultimately mounted with everyone cheering 'Al Hamdulilah.'

In excitement, Fatima kicked the horse on its sides, causing it to gallop into the fields. As the horse steadily sped up, she held on tightly, yelling and looked frightened to death. Arief couldn't help but laugh. Fatima waved when she saw Arief and the others clapping. That day, he was determined to marry this woman no matter what.

Arief shortly after approached her with the stride of confidence - a sure, steady gait. At first, she didn't say anything, taking her inquiries about 'this handsome man' to those who knew Arief well. It was only short while before they began falling in love. He learned she was born in Kuala Lumpur but was full-Indonesian. Fatima completed her Masters in Agricultural Science before returning to Jakarta.

Arief held unto the portrait tighter and didn't care to let go even if it would break in his hands. He reminisced about their first kiss during Idul Adha. As joyous as Fatima was always, she talked to his uncle about organising a party for both families and he loved the idea.

Even his late uncle had encouraged him to marry the girl for more than her beauty. He advised Arief know her spiritually, mentally... even as Arief's uncle heard his own words, they laughed knowing better. Arief never understood why his uncle had bad luck with women. Every time his uncle gave the Friday sermon about marriage, Arief laughed internally while having a serious face. He knew his uncle well; knowing that he was in his fifth marriage and counting.

The Idul Party was beautiful and beyond what Arief expected. Fatima had also organised a short play about the story of Hajar, Ismael and Ibrahim and placed its roles in the hands of the younger family members. The storytelling brought tears to the eyes of both families. But as soon as the the play was over, the real party had begun.

One would never believe the same family members that just acted solemn roles would be the ones who started playing rock and roll. Fatima and

Arief excused themselves and took a stroll down to the field towards the horses' stall.

It is where the kiss happened between Arief and Fatima which was so magical. They didn't think about how and why; Fatima's back was against the barn's wall and Arief leaned in. The kiss was deep; tongue on tongue, as they swallowed each other. When the horses neighed; they jumped as if someone had caught them.

"I'm sorry."

"No need to be. I'm yours from this day onward."

It was like everything happened just yesterday and no one who could take Arief's wife place; not his daughter, not the busty lady who constantly made passes at him at the mechanic shop, absolutely no one. "If only Imtiyaaz wouldn't have been born, Fatima wouldn't have died," Arief kept believing. "The child should have died instead," he once blurted to the eighteen-year-old Imtiyaaz. Unfortunately, every one in the neighborhood felt his brunt of his grief, not only Imtiyaaz.

CHAPTER 4

A week before Imtiyaaz left, she sat in her room as her father was preparing for work, wondering what'll happen if she didn't find a real job soon. She was feeling hungry when she heard the '*You Got Mail*' *notification*. That sound became all too familiar and lazily, Imtiyaaz took her time in finding out who had emailed her this time. A whimper of hope dawned when she opened it.

Dear Ms Imtiyaaz Arief,

Congratulations on your successful application to our recruiting agency in Dubai. We're delighted to offer you employment at...

Imtiyaaz didn't wait to read the rest before she screamed. She went down in prostration thanking

Allah for favouring her with this blessing. Her room was so tight that there wasn't any room to really celebrate. She went from screaming to laughing, back and forth. Then, Imtiyaaz jumped and pumped her fists in the air before sanity brought her back to the environs that she was still at Ayah's house. As much as he demanded quietness, it still probably wasn't enough and that was difficult for the young Imtiyaaz. She pulled out her phone and texted the only person who'd be excited to hear her good news; Sayyid Yacob.

Minutes later after he didn't reply, Imtiyaaz went down to the kitchen to tell her father.

"Ayah, I got an email for a job working in a hotel in the UAE." As joy brought the words out, fear also seeped in.

"That's why you were screaming? A job in the UAE?"

"Yes, Ayah. I'm sorry for disturbing you. I was just happy, Al-Hamdulilah." Her facial expression took a nosedive from her father's reaction.

"Congratulations, Imtiyaaz Arief. May Allah bless you always." Imtiyaaz went up to hug her father and it was awkward. She didn't know he'd be okay with it but it seems so. *Perhaps, he now would have his space to revere Fatima.*

"Ameen. Terimah Kasih, Papa."

"Sama-sama."

As the week went on, Imtiyaaz prepared for her big trip. Arief had given her his blessing and surprised her with buying the airline ticket. He didn't give her the chance to rejoice when he complained about Imtiyaaz oversleeping for Fajr two days in a row, It didn't take long before they were back to their old ways. Still, Arief tried. Night in, night out, he prayed to Allah to become a better father but his stubbornness blocked him from understanding his daughter. The silly disputes between them often ended in short shouting matches and Imtiyaaz knew that only her father had the power to change himself.

Imtiyaaz couldn't wait for the day she'd be flying out. She desired to live on her own and didn't tell people at the coffee shop she was leaving until three days before. When she did, everyone was shocked. In the meantime, her friend Hamid was on another adventure, in another country she never heard of. She left him a message on Facebook but he didn't respond. Also some were happy for Imtiyaaz, there were others who tried discouraging her. They told her she wasn't ready, too young and should be patient with the jobs in Indonesia – it was only a matter of time before she'll find something good. Her boss, Mr Razzaq wasn't happy one bit because his coffee shop was losing their best employee. He believed that by Imtiyaaz leaving, his business would collapse and many thought the same.

During Imtiyaaz's last day, she made sure to leave a good impression with the customers and told them to keep their loyalty to the business. Some assured her that they'd stick around, while others were indifferent; acknowledging that the shop wouldn't be the same without her.

The night before she left, Imtiyaaz could hardly sleep. Arief could hear her tossing and turning. He smiled as he remembered when he was around her age and travelled outside the country for the first time. But this wasn't about him. It was about a girl about to sail on a voyage where she had no idea where the ship's sail would take her. So, sleep came and luckily for Arief, tonight's dream held a note of promise to it.

In the morning as they were leaving out the

house to the airport, Arief told Imtiyaaz that if she senses anything wrong to come home immediately. Imtiyaaz responded by saying, "Don't worry, Ayah. I'll be okay."

Arief drove to the airport in silence, punctuated only by the noise of traffic. Once she got out of his white truck, without her father's help, he didn't look back as she walked away. His only words were, "Salam alaykum. Call me when you arrive."

"Ok, Ayah. Wa alaykum as Salam."

Arief wished he'd given her another hug, just one time. He'd enjoyed the last one while it lasted, although he only thought of Fatima.

The scent of Imtiyaaz's perfume lingered behind in his truck. Even as Arief saw her walking further and further inside the terminal, the scent remained strong. For sure, his daughter wasn't Fatima, never was and never will be. Arief smiled finally, having the urge to yell his daughter's name, but he didn't. He only wished she'd see him smile; but it was too late. Turning the car's ignition on, Arief remained smiling. He wanted to sing but it was too early in the morning.

At that thought while sitting inside the Humvee, Imtiyaaz remembered her father's voice saying *"Call when you arrive."* She realised she'd left her phone in the bag in the blue car. She looked at the rear mirror and didn't see it trailing them which caused her to panic.

"Where's the blue car?" she thought before saying the actual words. She didn't want to disturb Mr Ismael but finally gave in.

"Wait, please. Where's the blue car with my bags?"

"I told you your stuffs are safe. Relax." Ismael's soft, calming voice now had a steel edge that drove terror down Imtiyaaz's spine.

"I need to call my father."

"You can once we arrive at your hotel room. We're not far. Your bags will be there before us. Please relax."

"Ok."

CHAPTER 5

"Wait here. One of my men will come meet you." Ismael had told Imtiyaaz when they'd stopped at a flat on the way. The dwelling was semi-furnished with portraits hanging on the wall of Dubai's relics and had a broken air conditioner. The fan was blowing hot air, so Imtiyaaz turned it off. She then went to the bathroom and splashed water on her face. *Why haven't my bags arrived yet?* Pacing back and forth, Imtiyaaz wanted to know why they stopped. After standing, then sitting a few times, Imtiyaaz finally laid back on the bed causing it to creak even though she was petite.

Imtiyaaz began thinking about home once more; picturing everyone she'd ever come in contact with, wondering if they miss her or want her back. "Why am I here?" she pondered. Her reasons were perfectly scripted since she began applying straight out of high school starting with *work, then university, after that a better paying job, and finally marrying someone rich back home or if she was lucky, one of the Arabs.* Imtiyaaz made sure she'd stored these in her notes on her iPhone. If she lost focus, she'd open them reminding herself to not lose faith. But the future she'd planned up to now seems in this heat that will not be easy.

If I work hard for the next year or two, or at most three, I should be able to save enough money for a car. I should start learning how to drive soon. It shouldn't be that hard. Mr Ismael can help me. This should be easy for him.

After telling herself this over and over, Imtiyaaz started grinning. Her mind was filled with exaggerated dreams of her fancy car driving up Shaikh Zayed Road when her friends come to visit.

***

Two loud bangs on the door broke her peace. Imtiyaaz rushed to the door, finding two men. She couldn't tell if they were Arabs or Asians.

"You're Imtiyaaz, right?" asked one with an accent she was getting familiar with since she arrived earlier. "They're Arab," she thought.

"Yes."

They were dressed in white clothing resembling the high-classed businessmen of the Persian Gulf and one man was wearing sunglasses. *Why are they wearing these long garments in such heat? Any why is this man was wearing sunglasses at night?*

"It's time," said the man wearing sunglasses.

"Time for what?"

"Work."

"But..." Imtiyaaz pouted, wanting to change but her bags hadn't arrived yet. She wanted to shower and couldn't without changing. Though she said, "Okay, give me a few minutes to freshen up, please. And what's the deal with air conditioner not working?"

The men looked at each other in unison and one said, "I'm sorry for that. I'll tell the hotel management." Imtiyaaz felt their eyes lingering on her figure in a way she found obscene. They were staring as she turned around, ogling her rear end.

Why is this job starting right now? What about the training? Will there be a professional addressing a room full of eager youngsters wanting to learn the tricks and nuances of the hospitality industry?

Imtiyaaz tried remembering if Mr Ismael said anything else about the job in the email but there was very little time to think. With the men waiting in the other room, she hurried, so she wouldn't be late for her first day.

Ten minutes later, Imtiyaaz and the men were inside an SUV heading towards Downtown Dubai. The lights on Shaykh Zayed Road were beautiful, and the destination on the GPS indicated they were fifteen minutes away. However, because of traffic, the roads were jammed until they got to an area known as Riqqa.

The SUV pulled into a parking lot of *Al Hamid's Lounge & Restaurant*. The facade didn't look modern just a sprawling complex with had the look of low-budget rooms.

Imtiyaaz wanted to ask if this is where she will be working. From their visage, she knew they were not the people in charge. Once inside, Imtiyaaz and the men walked past the reception area and down a long hallway. The receptionist looked at Imtiyaaz in a such a leering way; staring at her as if she was a lamb being taken to a slaughterhouse. Imtiyaaz heard the sounds of rap music coming from one room as they were passing by and the hall was saturated with the smell of cigarettes. Imtiyaaz knew Arabs like to smoke, hearing the many hookah adventures that her Hamid had spoken of. He told Imtiyaaz he knew how to make different things from the smoke which she couldn't imagine.

They stopped in front of a room and the man wearing the sunglasses pulled out a key card. How the door opened with the sound of a click thrilled Imtiyaaz. She was happy to find something so trivial even in the tired state she was in. When they stepped inside, the smell of cigarettes got stronger. *This room was not used long ago. I wonder why.*

There was a simple bed, a dresser and TV which resembled the one she had back home. Imtiyaaz wondered why they were here and couldn't wait to leave. She looked at the men who stared at her blankly and made a hand gesture trying to get their attention.

"So, why are we here?"

"Just wait. Someone will come by in a little while. Make sure you freshen up," said the man wearing sunglasses as his partner began leaving.

The message was cryptic as much as the blank look on their faces. Before she could say anything else, the man told her don't worry and closed the door.

"Oh my God! They forgot to leave the keycard" gasped Imityaaz, two minutes after the men were long gone.

Imtiyaaz sighed, laying on the bed but was grateful that this place had air conditioning. She paced around the room, peeping at the ashtray with crushed cigarettes. One was still burning. *I wonder why.*

The walls in the room were painted bright yellow and the paint was peeled off in a few places. There was a smoky red light above but two lamps below lit up the room. She knew if she didn't get up off the bed, the combination of the lights, fatigue and slight hunger would make her sleepy. Imtiyaaz didn't want to leave a bad impression on her new employer.

About thirty minutes later, the door beeped and opened. A tall muscular man came inside, resembling an Indian but dressed in the white clothing like the Arabs with a cloth wrapped around his head. His beard was greying and eyes were black.

"Hello." His accent confirmed he's Indian.

"Hi."

"You're the new girl, right?" he asked smiling.

"Yes, sir. That's me." Imtiyaaz answered smiling back. "Is this where I will be staying for the training? I mean are the others staying at this hotel as well?"

The man ignored Imtiyaaz and stepped out of his black leather expensive-looking sandals. He then removed his head scarf, revealing his balding head-line and shortly after began removing his white garment, revealing his boxers underneath.

And his manhood stood out, and the sight of him now naked frightened Imtiyaaz.

"What's going on here? You have the wrong room, buddy."

The man said nothing as he walked towards Imtiyaaz. "Well, I've paid for you for the night and I appreciate if we can get down to business."

Imtiyaaz backed up until she was up against a wall, trapped.

"Paid money for me? For what? This has to be a mistake. I'm here to work in a hotel and just came a few hours ago."

"I don't care about that. This is the work you're

here to do tonight. So, do you want to do this gently or rough?"

"This is a mistake sir. Please, I have papers to prove what I'm telling you. I need to call the recruiter, Mr. Ismael."

The man stood above her. His bulky physique overshadowed her petiteness. He folded his arms like a schoolteacher about to lose his cool. When Imtiyaaz ended her sentence, the man reached to grab her and she pushed him away. The man slapped her and its sting forced her to the ground. He then threw her on top of the bed. Pinning her down, he ripped Imtiyaaz's clothing off, layer by layer like an animal attacking its prey. Imtiyaaz tried fighting but it was no use. He was too strong.

She sobbed, thinking about the warnings her friends told her as this was happening right before her very eyes. The man started pulling her panties down and Imtiyaaz tried to resist. He parted her legs as she kept kicking. One of his hands cupped her breasts, moving from one to the other.

She yelled as the Indian put his manhood inside. Imtiyaaz continued yelling as he went in and out, in and out. He kept saying *"Yallah, Yallah!"* Then he pulled his penis out and turned Imtiyaaz around. He stuck it inside and it hurt. Imtiyaaz pleaded but it seemed to give him more energy. For ten minutes, it felt like hell and it ended when she felt him having an orgasm that rock him. He finished and stood up up from her. His sweaty dark face was a horror to see.

Imtiyaaz had never felt so useless. Nothing her father did compared to how she was just taken like a piece of meat. Imtiyaaz shook violently as she cried, holding the sheet in the corner. As the man got dressed, he reached inside his overgarment and tossed a few bills at her. Imtiyaaz had seen this scene play out before on American movies; *a man tossing money on a prostitute he had sex with and leaving.*

Only the prostitutes didn't cry and Imtiyaaz was no prostitute. When the man left, the door beeped and Imtiyaaz then realised that this was the job that she was promised.

CHAPTER 6

Hours later, the door beeped again an opened; causing Imtiyaaz to wake up. She didn't know when she had fallen asleep. The memories of what had happened came back and she cried again. The two men who had brought her to the hotel were the ones there this time.

"She's a virgin. Yallah!" one of them yelled.

She jumped from the bed, rushing towards them screaming and tearing with all her might.

"I hate you! Fuck you! I want to go home! I want to go home!" This was the first time Imtiyaaz has ever cursed and it was a situation befitting nevertheless.

The men grabbed her and tried pinning her

down. She was not going to let what happened, happen again and kicked one of them in the nuts; causing the man to double over. Then, she kneed him in the face and he yelled. Neither had expected the fierceness of this young, sweet-looking Indonesian girl. Her ferocity took them by surprise. The other man grabbed her arm and she wriggled it away while head-butting him and kicking him in the nuts as well. The young girl heard him howl as she bit him; making him release her. He held his head lying on the floor as the other. Imtiyaaz ran to the door which was surprising left open and dashed down the hall.

"Help me! Help me!" she shouted as she ran inside the reception area.

There were older Arab ladies dressed in black seated in the lobby and the scantily-dressed Asian girl with tousled hair had startled them. Imtiyaaz pleaded for anyone to protect her.

One of the men came out the room and down the hall, holding his manhood. Imtiyaaz ran out of Hamid's front entrance into the blinding hot sun of Dubai's morning.

"Halt!" a voice with much authority yelled.

She didn't listen and kept running. The cars on the road were swerving, trying to avoid hitting her.

"I'm a police officer. Leave that girl alone!"

Imitiyaaz realised that the first command was not for her. She stopped and turned around. An officer dressed in the country's uniform with a baton and handcuffs hanging from his waist was talking with the man who was running after her. Imtiyaaz didn't know whether to keep running into the hot busy street or stop.

Escaping was of no use as this police officer was here to protect and serve me and would make an arrest. If I run, they may charge me as a prostitute and it wouldn't be long before Mr Ismael found me.

Imtiyaaz pondered as she gingerly walked back towards the officer who was yelling at her pursuer.

"You're going with me to the police station. Yallah!"

The officer placed both of them into a fancy green and white police car where the officer's partner was already seated up front. It took some convincing for Imtiyaaz to sit next to the man who tried to rape her. When the officers saw her reluctance, the officer handcuffed the man though it didn't make her feel any safer.

"I came here to—" said Imtiyaaz before being interrupted.

"Please don't talk. You'll have time to say

anything you wish at the police station. Let us get you there first."

The station looked like how most police precincts Imtiyaaz had seen in movies. A wide concrete bar with police officers sitting like tellers in a bank, talking in Arabic. Some were dealing with an old woman's complaint.

Imtiyaaz was directed to a seat while her pursuer was taken inside which she presumed to be a jail cell.

A few minutes later, an officer at reception motioned for Imtiyaaz to come forward. When she got to the dividing concrete bar, a paper and pen were pushed to her to write down her complaints.

"I can explain it all," she said impatiently. "I came here to work for the Zayn Agency."

"Just write anything you have here. This is a police station, not the courts."

The tone with which the officer spoke to Imtiyaaz dampened her spirits, but she shrugged it off and took the pen. Once finished, the officer took it from her and went inside telling Imtiyaaz to have a seat. Imtiyaaz was tired, but pleased that the police was there to help. Imtiyaaz thought of what her friends and father might say if she returned home so shortly after leaving for greener pastures. Then she thought of the possibility of never returning, but sticking around till she found a real job. Surely, there must be other hotels who would hire her. Imtiyaaz saw over a dozen of them while they were driving from the airport.

She was drowning in thoughts when the officer who took her statement came back.

"Ms Imtiyaaz Arief? Come here, please."

She stood up and walked towards him, trying to read the expression on his face. It was blank as far as she could tell.

"I'll need your residency papers, passport and work contract."

Imtiyaaz was flabbergasted and angered.

"Did you read my statement at all?"

"I did."

"Then, you should have read where I said what happened?"

The officer took a long hard look at her as if she was speaking was out of line.

"And you want me to take you at face value against this local citizen?"

"Yes. And you must find Mr Ismael of Zayn Agency and question him! I was raped at that hotel!"

"First of all, Ms Arief. There is no Zayn Agency in the entire GCC. At least, nothing that is registered, meaning it doesn't exist. Number two, this is the UAE, there is a Mr Ismael on every street. The name is so common, so we don't have enough information unless you provide us with more.

Imtiyaaz stood shaking her head. "What the hell are you good for? I'm a woman who's just been sexually assaulted and you're telling me you can't find the man in charge of bringing me here."

"Look, Ms Arief. I understand what you're going through. So, you see why I need you to produce your documents. And please stop talking. Your voice is giving me a headache. We have thousands of ladies like you coming up with tales like this every day staying in our country illegally." The officer felt vindicated as he attempted to make Imtiyaaz look young and dumb.

Imtiyaaz suddenly felt her stomach sink in. But still had a flash of hope when she thought about the man they were holding.

"Oh! What about the man that tried to rape me? He probably works for Mr Ismael and will know how to get in touch with him."

The officer smiled sadly.

"The local has been released after questioning.

He said he came to the hotel to get a massage and after paying you, you attacked him and ran away. An officer went back to the hotel room after you both came and found money on the bed. It was the exact amount he said he paid you."

"No! That's not true. I – I – I..." her voice trailed off.

"I'm afraid, Ms Arief, you have wasted the time of the police and have made us arrest an innocent local man. The officer who brought you in is outside to take you back to where he picked you from. We can arrest you for filing a false report but we'll give you a second chance."

"What?"

"Dressed in that type of clothing, you're a person who make the holy men of this country fall into sin. May God forgive you. You may leave now."

Imtiyaaz was taken away out of the police station. She didn't struggle. She was too weak. Too defeated and broken. And was too numb to even cry.

Minutes later, Imtiyaaz was dropped off at Hamid's, completely dumbfounded, emptied of all emotions. On the bed, she found a red fishnet top and lacy bra, with black bum shorts and high black boots. She had seen this before; the universal regalia of a prostitution ring.

During the first week, there was nightmare after nightmare. Men of all sizes came to the room and used her in very callous ways. She was not permitted to go anywhere outside. The guards in front was paid off to keep watch on her and the same police officer who found her was bribed. No phone or internet was inside the room. Imtiyaaz had no way of contacting anyone. The men brought all she needed in terms of clothes and cosmetics. Three times a day, someone brought food in and quickly locked the door. Imtiyaaz realised there were other Asian women at the hotel and men were paying for their services. She heard the voices of women talking in Malay, Chinese, Hindi, Vietnamese, Cambodian and other languages when she wasn't occupied, restricted to the lobby or lounge area. Inside the hallways, there were only sounds of sex activity on the 5th floor, day and night. Hamid's was running an underground operation of sex trafficking and there wasn't anything no one could do about it. Whenever she asked about Mr Ismael, they told her they don't know who she's talking about.

One man watched her cry after intercourse. Imtiyaaz just laid feeling useless.

"What's wrong, my daughter?" he asked.

Imtiyaaz was surprised as no one had ever spoken to her with such tone. The men that came had a high sex drive. Imtiyaaz can feel it in their loins when they ejaculated. They left feeling relieved after emptying themselves inside her.

Imtiyaaz told the man of her plight as he listened attentively. When Imtiyaaz finished talking, his reply was "this is a one-way journey. There's no getting out. Every sex worker you see here either leaves the work old or dead. No one gets out. You have to be strong. No one will help you in this country. Your kindness is looked down on as less than human. I advise you to make peace with your Lord and not just lie there. Enjoy the sex and money that has been granted to you. You'll be old soon."

Imtiyaaz felt like beating the skinny man to a pulp. He was clearly a sadist. *What a freak!*

A month and a half passed by and Imtiyaaz felt herself being hollowed out with every man that passed through her.

The weekends were the worse. She was either being fucked in threesomes or crying herself silly waiting for the next customer who she hoped would be only one. One of the Asian girls offered Imtiyaaz drugs, but she refused, citing she needed what sanity she had left if she was to get out of here alive.

Imtiyaaz thought about escaping but she didn't have her passport nor enough money. She came up with a plan after the last client for the evening.

"Wake up. I'm here to clean the room."

The cleaner shook Imtiyaaz and had been doing so for the past minute. The Indian lady wondered what kind of sleep is this? She blurted, "must have been another busy night."

Then, she shook Imtiyaaz violently and found Imtiyaaz, barely breathing.

Sensing something was wrong when she glanced over, seeing pills scattered on the bed. The cleaner ran out and raced to the receptionist.

"I think the girl in Room 740 tried to kill herself. She's unconscious. There are painkillers all over her bed."

The receptionist pulled out his cell phone and dialled.

"Your Indonesian tried to kill herself. Send a doctor."

"Tayyib," said the man on the other end of the line.

CHAPTER 7

Twelve hours later, Mr Ismael had enough time to weigh his options. He told the receptionist and cleaner to keep this to themselves, paying them 10000 dirhams in exchange. If word got out that one of the girls tried to commit suicide, there would be no telling what the others might do and Mr Ismael would certainly be out of business. Every girl was sponsored by a local in his network and had to make sure their investments were kept intact.

Ismael started this human trafficking ring ten years ago and had used college students like Aisyah to find naïve and ambitious young girls to recruit from countries of Asia and Africa. They'd tricked the girls with job offers in different sectors of retail, tourism and other related fields, knowing they would have full control over their residency statuses. If they didn't comply, they'd label them as prostitutes and report them to the police. Most gave in but there were a few that escaped and were deported after serving their jail terms. In this particular situation involving Imtiyaaz, Ismael had a soft spot. *Why would this young woman want to take her life and she could make so much money living here and not back home getting peanuts?*

On the drive to the hotel from Rashidiyah, Mr Ismael considered cutting his losses with Imtiyaaz and letting her go back home but needed to talk with her further before doing so.

Better to lose out on one bad apple than allowing it to ruin the bunch? His sponsors would be in trouble if one of the girls had died from drugs. The country's laws are very strict on illegal drugs and anyone was found distributing or consuming, would be executed without hesitation.

"What do you want, Imtiyaaz? More money? Or hell back home?" asked Ismael who finally arrived to Hamid's in a bid to keep things under wraps.

Imtiyaaz's eyes focused on the man who had caused her to lose her virginity. She cursed the days of Aisyah telling her about this ruse of a ghost businesses. To Imtiyaaz, Aisyah deserved more blame than Ismael. She acted as a sister to her, always encouraging to go and do the right thing. If it wasn't for her, Imtiyaaz wouldn't have emailed Mr Ismael for the hotel jobs.

"I want to go home. I just want to go home. Please."

"If you wait for a few more months, you'll pay off your fees and then you can do whatever you like."

"No. If you wait a few more days, you'll find me dead. I'm not joking. Please release me."

"You're in no position to make any demands, my lady. I have everything you need including this job. Bear with me and I'll take care of you," said Ismael calmly.

"I ask you by Allah because I know you're Muslim to do the right thing. My father will kill me if he finds out that this happened. I'll never say a word. Please."

After a minute of pondering, Ismael told Imtiyaaz to pack whatever she had and meet him outside. They would be heading to the Dubai International Airport.

As Imtiyaaz walked through airport security with just a carryon holding her stained jacket, the bags under her eyes showed a woman in desperate need of help. She was brimming with tears when an immigration officer asked her how was her stay in the UAE. He took it as a compliment that she was overjoyed but that wasn't the case.

How Imtiyaaz survived almost 3 months in these circumstances was a miracle? What would have happened if she had died from the painkillers that night? Did Arief ever tried to contact her? Imtiyaaz will only know when she arrive back it Jakarta. Her cell phone isn't charged and her things are locked away in the baggage department beneath the plane. She knew at least Yacob would have tried.

In thirteen hours, she'll find out if what she left behind in Jakarta was the better option. The young woman by the name of Imtiyaaz Arief is widely known to many human trafficking rescue organizations. All are heroes like Imtiyaaz despite some escaping and some who still have not.

With only her freedom, Imtiyaaz realised, that the value of it was more than anything else in the world.

AFTERWORD

Trafficking is a serious problem that all countries need to address; providing real dialogue and community healing in order in doing so. The rich prey on the poor and the strong prey on the weak, thus leading to a global epidemic that all humanity need to stand up against.

If you enjoyed this story, please email me at feekness@gmail.com with your testimonial.